Dora and the Baby Crab

by Kirsten Larsen   illustrated by Robert Roper

Ready-to-Read

Simon Spotlight/Nick Jr.
New York   London   Toronto   Sydney

Based on the TV series *Dora the Explorer*® as seen on Nick Jr.®

SIMON SPOTLIGHT
An imprint of Simon & Schuster Children's Publishing Division
1230 Avenue of the Americas, New York, New York 10020
© 2008 Viacom International Inc. All rights reserved.
NICK JR., *Dora the Explorer*, and all related titles, logos, and characters are
registered trademarks of Viacom International Inc. All rights reserved, including the right
of reproduction in whole or in part in any form. SIMON SPOTLIGHT, READY-TO-READ, and colophon are
registered trademarks of Simon & Schuster, Inc.
Manufactured in the United States of America

6 8 10 9 7

Library of Congress Cataloging-in-Publication Data
Larsen, Kirsten.
Dora and the baby crab / by Kirsten Larsen ; illustrated by Robert Roper.
—1st ed.
p. cm. — (Ready-to-read)
"Based on the TV series Dora the Explorer, as seen on Nick Jr."—T.p.
verso.
ISBN-13: 978-1-4169-5451-4
ISBN-10: 1-4169-5451-1
0111 LAK
I. Roper, Robert. II. Dora the explorer (Television program)
III. Title.
PZ7.L323817Do 2008
2007026222

Hi! I am  .

DORA

Today  and I

BOOTS

are at the  .

BEACH

Oh, no!

 is caught in a .

BABY CRAB · NET

He needs our help!

We need something

to cut through the .

NET

We can look in  .
BACKPACK

Do you see something

that can cut through the ? NET

These  SCISSORS

can cut through the NET !

 has a .

BABY CRAB   SHELL NECKLACE

He wants to give it

to  .

MAMI CRAB

But he cannot find her.

We can help him

find .
MAMI CRAB

 is on .
MAMI CRAB   CRAB ISLAND

To get to ,

CRAB ISLAND

we need to go through

the

SAND CASTLE

and over the  .

SNAPPING CLAMS

Come on!

We made it to the .
SAND CASTLE

What a nice  !
SAND CASTLE

I wonder who lives here.

The  lives here!

The SQUISHY SQUID

The SQUISHY SQUID likes to play

music.

To go through the ,
SAND CASTLE

we have to sing and dance

to the 's song.
SQUISHY SQUID

We did it!

We made it through

the . SAND CASTLE

Great!

Where do we go next?

Yeah!

We go over the .

SNAPPING CLAMS

The  are big.

SNAPPING CLAMS

And they snap!

How do we get over them

without getting snapped?

When the  snap,

SNAPPING CLAMS

we have to jump.

Jump!

Jump!

Jump over the  !

SNAPPING CLAMS

Look! There is  .
CRAB ISLAND

We can use this BOAT

to get there.

Uh-oh.

The are missing!
OARS

We cannot paddle the
BOAT

without .
OARS

BABY CRAB can help us.

He is pulling the  **BOAT** !

Wow, he is pulling fast!

 is strong.

BABY CRAB

We made it to !
CRAB ISLAND

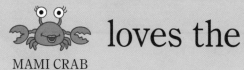 loves the .
MAMI CRAB   SHELL NECKLACE

She loves , too!
BABY CRAB